My Cat

Katie Gillespie

EYEDISCOVER

EYEDISCOVER

Go to **www.eyediscover.com** and enter this book's unique code.

BOOK CODE

X975892

EYEDISCOVER brings you media enhanced books that support active learning.

Published by AV² by Weigl
350 5th Avenue, 59th Floor New York, NY 10118
Website: www.eyediscover.com

Library of Congress Control Number: 2016932936

ISBN 978-1-4896-5169-3 (hardcover)

Printed in the United States of America in Brainerd, Minnesota
1 2 3 4 5 6 7 8 9 0 20 19 18 17 16

032016
030416

Editor: Katie Gillespie
Designer: Mandy Christiansen

Weigl acknowledges Getty Images, iStock, Corbis, Alamy, Minden, and Shutterstock as the primary image suppliers for this title. Page 1: Addy Gladstone.

EYEDISCOVER provides enriched content, optimized for tablet use, that supplements and complements this book. EYEDISCOVER books strive to create inspired learning and engage young minds in a total learning experience.

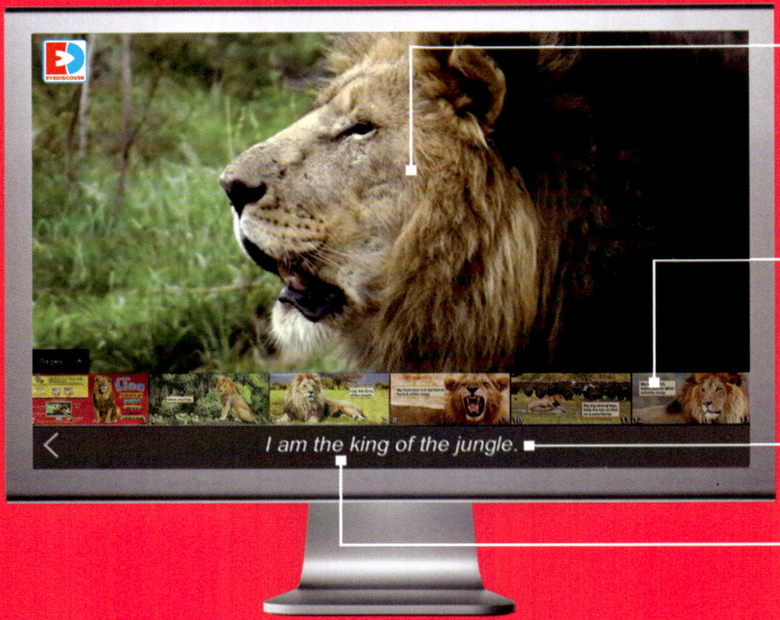

Watch
Video content brings each page to life.

Browse
Thumbnails make navigation simple.

Read
Follow along with text on the screen.

Listen
Hear each page read aloud.

Your EYEDISCOVER Media Enhanced books come alive with...

Audio
Listen to the entire book read aloud.

Video
High resolution videos turn each spread into an optic readalong.

OPTIMIZED FOR

- ☑ TABLETS
- ☑ WHITEBOARDS
- ☑ COMPUTERS
- ☑ AND MUCH MORE!

My Cat

In this book, you will learn about

- what she eats
- how I care for her
- what she does

and much more!

I love my cat.

My pet kitten was very small when she was born. She drank milk for about eight weeks.

Cats sleep for about 15 hours every day. My pet cat takes many naps.

Cats can jump very high. My cat can leap right over our fence.

My cat eats two times a day. I give her both wet and dry food.

Cats lick their fur to groom themselves. They use their rough tongues like combs.

My cat likes it when I brush her fur. This also helps to keep her clean.

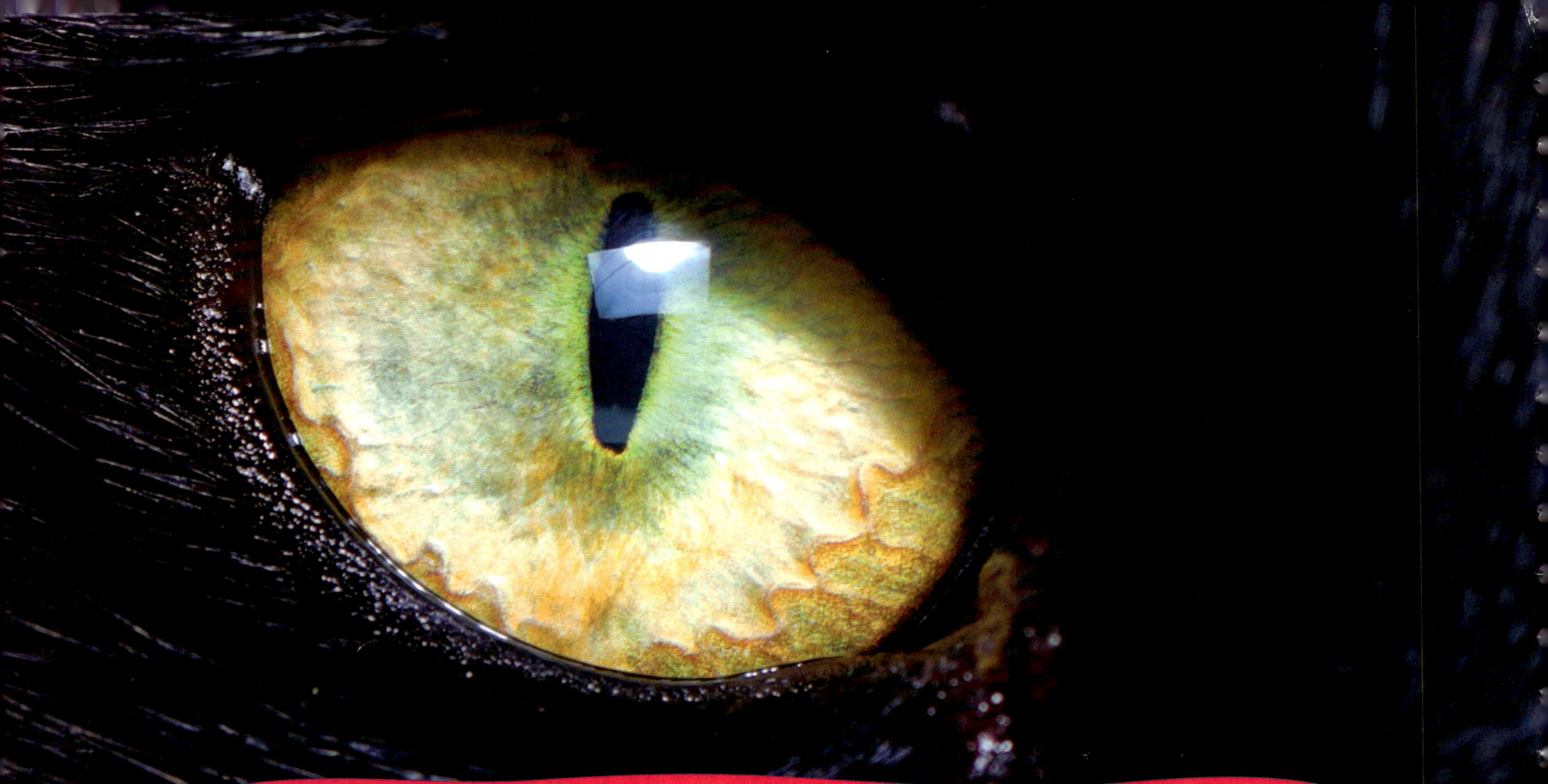

My cat can see well at night.
Her eyes glow in the dark.

Cats need regular checkups. The veterinarian makes sure my cat stays healthy.

CATS BY THE NUMBERS

Cats **sweat** through their **PAWS.**

Cats have **32** muscles in **each** ear.

A cat can run up to 30 miles per hour.
(50 kilometers per hour)

Bella is the **#1** **most popular** cat name in the **United States.**

House cats share 95.6% of their DNA with TIGERS.

There are at least 74 million pet cats in the United States.

Cats **walk** and **run** on their

T O E S.

KEY WORDS

Research has shown that as much as 65 percent of all written material published in English is made up of 300 words. These 300 words cannot be taught using pictures or learned by sounding them out. They must be recognized by sight. This book contains 46 common sight words to help young readers improve their reading fluency and comprehension. This book also teaches young readers several important content words, such as proper nouns. These words are paired with pictures to aid in learning and improve understanding.

Page	Sight Words First Appearance
4	I, my
6	about, for, she, small, very, was, when
8	day, every, many, takes
11	can, high, our, over, right
12	a, and, both, eats, food, give, her, times, two
14	like, their, they, to, use
17	also, helps, it, keep, this
18	at, eyes, in, night, see, the, well
20	makes, need

Page	Content Words First Appearance
4	cat
6	kitten, milk
8	naps
11	fence
14	combs, fur, tongues
18	dark
20	checkups, veterinarian

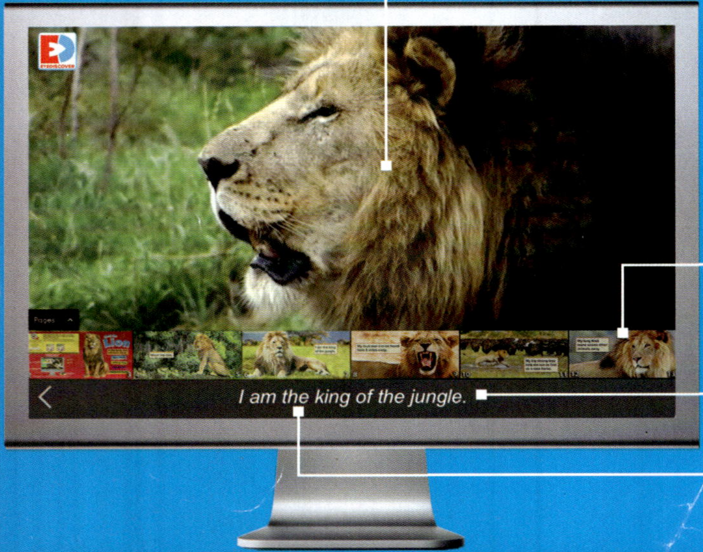

Watch
Video content brings each page to life.

Browse
Thumbnails make navigation simple.

Read
Follow along with text on the screen.

Listen
Hear each page read aloud.

EYEDISCOVER

Go to www.eyediscover.com and enter this book's unique code.

BOOK CODE

X975892